My Friend the Enemy

Dedicated with love to
my favorite big brother,
Dr. Richard Phillips, from Doris.

MY FRIEND, THE ENEMY
© 1992 by A Corner of the Heart

Published by Multnomah Press Books
P.O. Box 1720
Sisters,Oregon 97759

Printed in the United States of America.

Questar Publishers, Inc.
Post Office Box 1720
Sisters, Oregon 97759

My Friend the Enemy

SURVIVING A PRISON CAMP

BY DORIS SANFORD

ILLUSTRATIONS BY GRACI EVANS

MULTNOMAH PRESS

Something was wrong. It had been wrong for days. Too many adults whispering, too many children clinging and crying, too many teachers looking worried. It was Kathy's first year at school and her first time to live away from Mother and Daddy. It helped having Dick, her big brother, here at the boarding school. It didn't help that their parents were hundreds of miles away in the north part of the country. She remembered Mother saying that it would be safer for them at school. China was on the verge of war.

The day the Japanese soldiers came, Kathy felt very unsafe. The soldiers herded and pushed the children to the front gate, yelling in a language that no one understood. It was good they didn't know all that was ahead! At that moment all they knew was that they were being sent to live somewhere else. They didn't know where, or why, or how long they would stay.

After days of long, hard walking the 1,700 adults and children arrived at a dirty compound. Kathy was five years old and Dick was ten years old when they became prisoners-of-war in this concentration camp in China. It didn't take long to figure out that living here was not the best place to be. It was also clear that they didn't have any choice. Soldiers with guns are always the boss.

Life changed for them that day. For the next five years they would live in an area the size of two football fields. Thieves, doctors, street women, teachers, and school children all would live together. Gone were the cozy dorm rooms, the linens and fresh flowers at dinner, the playground equipment, and toilets that flushed. Everyone slept only inches from the next person on the floor or on top of trunks. They slept, dressed, washed, and lived every minute of the day in full view of everyone else.

In the winter their pillows froze solid in the unheated warehouse buildings. To keep their toes from freezing, the children sat with their feet in cardboard boxes filled with hay.

Their beds, full of dirt and soot from the coal balls they carried to the cooking area each day, were overrun with bedbugs. Some adults called the bedbugs "China's millions." Some of the children kept them in bottles as pets. Kathy was sure that a kitten would have been a better pet!

Large rats ran freely throughout the camp. The older children set up teams for rat-catching competitions, clubbing the rats with sticks. At the end of the day they lined up all the dead rats in the courtyard for the "count." The daily winner was then announced. Sixty-eight rats were the most caught in one day! When summer flies became too numerous to tolerate, the children organized fly-catching teams and stored the catch of the day in bottles. One of Dick's friends caught 3,500!

Kathy worried about running out of food. Sometimes there was only sour bread and water to eat. Other times bullies took more than their share. Most of the time the food was not worth fighting about. Breakfast, lunch, and dinner were called S.O.S. (the same old stew). It was made from boiled cattle feed and a soup made of garden weeds or rice, and a little tea. It had more worms than anything else. They were told the worms were God's gift to them since it was the only meat available and that they must be thankful. Kathy hoped that God never found out that she *wasn't* thankful. Apparently God didn't know that none of her friends liked worms.

The children in
the camp responded
to the war differently.
The boys played war
games. When they weren't
doing that, they made war
noises.

12

Kathy responded by finding a place to be alone. It wasn't easy to find, since other people also wanted such a place.

When she was alone, she loved to play "Let's pretend." Let's pretend it's Christmas and we are at home. Let's pretend the war is over. Let's pretend I could have any doll I wanted. Let's pretend I could have anything I wanted to eat.

Pretending helped a little. It also made her sad. Pretend was never as good as *real*. Later as her hunger grew, it was too painful to make a game about food and she merely thought about what she would eat someday.

The last two years Kathy was in the camp, she neither talked nor thought about food. It was more than even dreams could manage.

School came in bits and pieces. During the day the teachers taught school lessons when there was time between the children's endless chores. Kathy and Dick and the other children swept floors, washed dishes, and carried coal dust balls to the kitchen.

None of the jobs were fun, but some were less fun than others, and some even were dangerous.

Gathering eggs was one of those dangerous jobs. At night friends on the outside occasionally lowered eggs over the wall to a waiting child or adult. Sometimes they had to pay for the eggs. A wedding ring could buy several eggs. If a soldier caught someone receiving eggs, that person was shot. But the adults knew the children in the camp needed the eggs because their teeth were coming in without enamel. The adults would grind up the eggshells and feed them to the younger children because the shells contained calcium.

Every Sunday afternoon the children wrote letters to their parents. The letters were filled with questions: Will I ever see you again? Will I die? Why are we having this war? Later several teenagers found a pile of letters that were never mailed. The children knew then that the required letter writing had been merely to keep up their hopes.

Kathy and Dick had no contact with their parents, not even by letter, during the five years they were in the camp. But one day when a doctor was allowed into the camp to treat a soldier, he asked them to write their names, height, and weight on a tiny scrap of paper which then was taped to the inside of medicine labels on bottles filled with medicine and later shipped to their parents. This was the only message their parents ever received during the five years.

What was even more difficult was that Kathy and Dick lived in separate sections of the camp and for several years they were allowed to speak to each other only once a week.

Because of the lack of good food and medical care and the dirty living conditions, many adults and children in the camp died. The camp was full of people with dysentery, malaria, hepatitis, tuberculosis, and cholera. Kathy was sick much of the time. If there ever was a time when she longed for her parents to come and get her, it was when she was sick. If she only knew *when* this would end, she could bear it.

The daily schedule was rigid. There were few surprises. Knowing what would happen next helped Kathy feel secure. Morning began by breaking ice in a bucket and vigorously washing her face. This was followed by her teacher's inspection. Roll call occurred twice a day as well as any other time the soldiers decided to call roll—even at midnight.

Some of Kathy's friends had grown one foot since they'd been in the camp. "New" clothes were made from curtains, mattress covers, tablecloths, and sheets.

Whatever happened, the teachers' rules were clear. Complaining was not allowed and eating with a bent stick was no cause for poor table manners. It helped that the teachers seemed calm and matter of fact. Their solution to feeling lonely was, "Just don't think about it." Sometimes that worked, and sometimes it didn't.

Some nights Kathy's fears gave her nightmares and she wished just once that someone warm and soft would tuck her in, hug her, and tell her that everything would be all right. *Being brave is hard work!* The teachers told them that the Chinese word for *crisis* was a combination of two words: *danger* and *opportunity*. They told the children that they could choose to see either danger or opportunity in *any* situation. Kathy decided to do her best to see the opportunity in each day.

22

The hardest day of all came when she couldn't remember what her mother's face looked like. If that were true, then perhaps Mother wouldn't know her when they got out of the prison camp. But most days she didn't think such unhappy thoughts. They didn't make anything better.

The teachers also reminded the children that "the soldiers cannot take God out of this camp. He is locked up in here with us." They said it again and again. Kathy knew it was true. It helped when the teachers promised to always tell them the truth about what was happening in the war. Kathy found that she could forget almost anything for a little while by playing games, singing, and telling stories with happy endings.

One of the reasons Kathy and Dick survived the camp was because their parents had prepared them to survive. Their parents taught them to learn everything by heart because they never knew when they would be without music, books, poetry, and Bibles. It was because of this that Kathy learned all five verses to the song, "I Heard the Bells on Christmas Day." She loved to sing it, "Wild and sweet the words repeat, Of peace on earth, good will to men." One of the teachers would say, "Do what would make your parents proud of you." It worked every time; singing *would* make them proud.

Kathy knew they were not completely safe. No one ever said they were. She also knew that the adults were scared sometimes, but they said being scared in scary situations was normal. Kathy and Dick were told that they were the kind of children who have the strength to survive. It never occurred to them to doubt it. Singing and survival go together.

When there was no reason to celebrate, they created reasons. An occasional flower that grew in the compound wall, a butterfly that disobeyed the guard-tower warning and danced anyway were reasons enough to celebrate. Celebrations could be had for the asking.

Surprisingly, a friendship developed between Kathy and one of the soldiers. It started because the two liked to draw. They would meet behind the far building where no one would see them. While they drew in the dirt, Kathy hummed or sang, "I Heard the Bells on Christmas Day"—all five verses. When she got to the ending, she tilted her head back and sang until her voice cracked: "Wild and sweet the words repeat, Of peace on earth, good will to men." At first he hummed along and then slowly began to sing with her, just a word here and there. It always made Kathy want to laugh. She knew he didn't understand the meaning of the words, but that was okay. It became "their song."

Kathy learned through his drawings and hand signs that her soldier friend had a little girl about her age. When his daughter became very ill, Kathy secretly made her a small doll from the sleeve of one of her old dresses.

The soldier continued to yell at her whenever one of the "boss" guards watched him, but once she noticed that he had tears in his eyes after the boss left.

Finally the day they had all been waiting for came! A helicopter circled overhead and then with a cloud of dust landed in the middle of the courtyard. Seven Americans hopped out and yelled, "It's over! The war is over!" Every child and adult ran screaming, leaping, and laughing! Believe it or not, the war was over!

The war is over!

Kathy ran back to the barracks to get her doll. She saw her soldier friend. He was slumped against the wall with his head bowed low. She hugged him, and for the briefest moment, he forgot he was the enemy.

He jumped to his feet, and rule or no rule, they held hands and danced in a circle and sang: "Wild and sweet the words repeat, Of peace on earth, good will to men."

Discussion Questions

1. What do you think was the scariest part about being in the concentration camp?

2. What helped Kathy when she felt afraid?

3. Have you ever been in a very frightening experience? Tell about it.

4. In this story the Japanese and Americans were at war. Why do you think Kathy, an American child, and the Japanese soldier became friends?

5. What could you do to make peace when you are fighting with someone?

6. Why do countries have wars?

7. When you are afraid, what are some things you could do that would help you?